The Stone !  's

Written by Zoë Clarke

Illustrated by Edu Coll

Collins

2

"Wow!" Moe said.

Fade and Shade were the top Stone Shadows.

The Stone Shadows slept inside old boulders.

The Shadows helped people in peril.
And pets!

Moe went for training.
"You are not a Shadow!" said Fade.

"But I have *got* a shadow!" said Moe.
Shade nodded. "So you have."

"Train with Slate," Fade told Moe.
Shade sighed. "And Kevin."

"Do Shadows get capes and shields?"
"No ... and no," said Fade.

"Shadows are a team! Go for it! Reach that kite," Fade said.

Kevin fell over.

Slate hopped on Kevin's shoulders.

Moe jumped on Slate's shoulders.

"Shadows are quick! Show me!
Follow Fade," said Shade.

"Grab skates!" Moe said. "Hold on!"
Moe towed Kevin.
Kevin towed Slate.

"Shadows clean up!" said Fade.
They went into the cold stream.

"Can we save people in peril?" said Moe.
Fade said, "Pets next!"

"Save Squeak!" said Shade.
Kevin sighed. "That window is high up."

"Good job, team," Shade told them.

SPEED ✓

CLEAN UP ✓

SAVE PETS ✓

"*Now* can we help people in peril?" Moe said.

Zoom!

Kapow!

Splat!

"You *have* helped people," Fade told Moe.
"You ARE Stone Shadows!" said Shade.

The Stone Shadows!

Helping when people are not in peril!

Join the Stone Shadows!

HOP AND JUMP!

SKATE AND TOW!

CLEAN STREAMS!

THROW QUICK!

SAVE MOE AND SQUEAK!

HELP PEOPLE AND PETS!

After reading

Letters and Sounds: Phase 5

Word count: 249

Focus phonemes: /ai/ ey, a-e /ee/ ie, ea /igh/ i, i-e /oa/ o, oe, ow, ou, o-e

Common exception words: the, are, we, me, you, said, have, to, do, were, when, people, he, into

Curriculum links: PSHE

National Curriculum learning objectives: Reading/word reading: read accurately by blending sounds; read accurately by blending sounds in unfamiliar words containing GPCs that have been taught; read words containing taught GPCs; Reading/comprehension: understand both the books they can already read accurately and fluently and those they listen to by checking that the text makes sense to them as they read, and correcting inaccurate reading; making inferences on the basis of what is being said and done

Developing fluency

- Your child may enjoy hearing you read the book.
- Take turns to read a page. Demonstrate how to add emphasis for words in italics and capitals (pages 7, 19 and 20) and check your child adjusts their tone for sentences ending in exclamation and question marks.

Phonic practice

- Focus on the different ways in which the letter sound /oa/ is written. Ask your child to sound out the following but to look out for one word with the /ow/ sound:

    show   tiptoes   wow   tow   stone   go

- Ask your child to sound out the following. Which words have an /ow/ sound and which have an /oa/ sound?

    show   now   shadows   follow   window

Extending vocabulary

- Page 2 suggests that the Stone Shadows are **brave**. Ask your child to think of other words that describe the team too. (e.g. *tidy, kind, strong, quick, powerful, mysterious, confident*)
- The Shadows help people and pets in **peril**. Challenge your child to think of other words or phrases which have a similar meaning to peril. (e.g. *in danger, at risk, in difficulty*)